LOVING SEBASTIAN

Azalyn St. Francis

Thank you to my son Jared Lewis, my unpaid but still enthusiastic editor and always my biggest cheerleader

TABLE OF CONTENTS

Chapter 1

"You look amazing, Mom. Tawny, you are a genius," Ashley spoke to the makeup artist.

"You do look beautiful, Miss Rosie," Tawny said. "But it's not just the makeup. You are glowing. That inside beauty is shining through."

In a few minutes, Rosalinda Turner would be renewing her vows with Michael, her husband of 30 years. She was a stunning woman, 50 years old with caramel colored, flawless skin, a voluptuous body and luxurious jet-black hair. She was an Afro-Latina born in the Dominican Republic and raised in the Bronx. Her distinctive New York accent was still thick after almost 30 years in Texas.

"Please tell us the secret. How do you manage to stay in love with the same man for 30 years? How did you meet him?" Tawny asked.

"Meeting men doesn't seem to be our problem. It's holding on to one that's the issue," Ashley chimed in.

"You are so right, Sis. Good catch, no hold. That's the story of my life," Tawny said as she patted Rosalinda's face with a puff and stepped back to look at her handywork. She handed Rosalinda a hand mirror.

"I love it," Rosalinda said. "Good work, Tawny. I met my husband on the subway in the Bronx, New York. I stalked him for a week. The minute I saw him, I knew I had to have him."

"Oh my! This is rich. Spill the tea, Miss Rosie."

Ashley glanced at the clock on the dresser and decided not to intervene in her mother's tale. She would hurry her mother along in a minute, but she did not stop her. She had heard the story at least a hundred times but she never tired of hearing it. It was her family's origin story after all. She would listen one more time and then gather her mother to go downstairs where Ashley and her brother Brian would escort their mother down the aisle to repeat her wedding vows to the love of her life.

CHAPTER 2

osalinda saw the man on the train again. She'd missed him the day before, so she arrived 15 minutes earlier and saw him approaching the track as he always did. He was quite tall, over 6 feet, slender, and impossibly handsome. He had a smooth dark brown complexion and a neatly trimmed beard. He had to be a student. He wore jeans and t-shirts every day with well-worn tennis shoes. He carried a dark green backpack that looked like it had seen better days, a rolled-up newspaper in one hand and a cup of coffee in the other.

The man took a seat in the back while Rosalinda was forced to grab a strap and stand next to the door. She watched the man give his seat to another elderly man. He stood and approached her. He grabbed the strap next to and stood close enough for her to see the thickness of his eyelashes.

"I was hoping I'd see you here today," he said. "I won't be taking this train anymore. This is my last ride." He smiled at her with perfect teeth. He was easily a foot taller than she was, so he leaned in slightly to speak to her. He smelled of clean scented soap and coffee. She felt a shiver travel down her spine. "My name is Michael. What's yours?"

"Rosalinda. But everyone calls me Rosie."

"Rosie. That's a beautiful name," he said. "It suits you."

"Why is this your last ride?" she asked.

"I'm moving to Texas for grad school. I'm leaving in a month."

Rosie felt her heart sink. Too little. Too late. She thought.

"But look, I would love to buy you dinner before I leave. What do you think?" He reached into his backpack and pulled out a pen. He scribbled his name and number on the back of an index card with class notes on it and handed it her.

"Look, this is my stop. Promise me, you'll call me."

"I'll call you" Rosie said. Michael squeezed her hand as she held tightly onto the strap and then turned. The train doors closed behind him as he exited the train.

Two days later, Michael Turner knocked on the door of the two-bedroom apartment Rosie shared with her parents and her two sisters. Rosie had barely been able to contain herself at her job as a receptionist at an accounting office. She watched the clock more than usual and worried that the new haircut she spent a day's pay on would not be flattering.

Michael arrived in dress shirt and slacks and a sports jacket. Rosie wore a teal-colored dress, cinched at the waist with a full skirt. Rosie opened the door and invited him in. The apartment was small and decorated with the requisite icons of saints and family photos. Michael reached out to touch Rosie but then her mother came into the room.

"Hello, young man. Introduce us, Rosie. He's quite handsome."

"Mama, this is Michael Turner. Michael, this is my mother, Mrs. Olivares."

"It's a pleasure, Ma'am. It's easy to see where your daughter gets her beauty."

"Well, that's bullshit. But personally, I like bullshit." She had probably been quite lovely in her day, but it was easy to see from the lines on her face and the glass of brown liquid in her hand that life had not treated her well.

"Mama, please."

"Never mind me, Michael. Just go on. Have a good time you two."

Rosie kissed her mother on the cheek and took Michael's arm and led him out of the apartment.

At dinner Michael told Rosie that he had graduated from Columbia with a degree in Architecture. He'd been offered a scholarship and was moving to Houston, Texas to get a master's degree at Rice University. He was originally from Syracuse. He was excited about warm winters in Texas.

"I'd be more than happy never to see snow again," he said.

"I've never been any further away than New Jersey," Rosie said. "It sounds exciting."

"Then you have to come see me. Come to Texas. You should come with me." He held one of her hands in his. He looked so deeply into her eyes that she almost believed that she could. That she should.

Later they walked home from the restaurant hand in hand. Rosie kept looking up at him as he talked, thinking he might disappear if she didn't. When they started to feel a slight chill, Michael took off his jacket and pulled it around her shoulders. When they got to her stoop, she did not want him to leave.

"Can I see you tomorrow?" he asked. "And the next day too. I want to see you every night until I leave."

"Yes," she breathed. "I'll see you tomorrow." His kiss that night was sweet and gentle, leaving Rosie wanting more. He waited until she was safely in her apartment before he set off walking. She watched him from her window until she could no longer make him out at the corner.

The next night he came to her apartment. They were alone. Her parents were both at work. Her sisters out with friends.

The moment Michael entered the apartment, Rosie pulled him into her arms. She was a virgin, but she no longer wanted to be. She wanted Michael Turner to fuck her, and she was prepared for it. She plunged her tongue into this mouth and tasted the sweetness. In turn, he kissed her face, her neck, her shoulder blades. She could feel him growing hard against her body. She grew wetter and wetter until she thought her juices might run down her legs. She took Michael into the bedroom she shared with her sisters. They undressed quickly. Rosie had never been so close to a naked male body. She was not disappointed. Michael was dark and lean with smooth dark skin. His dick was rock hard and at full attention. She was so enamored of the gloriousness of his penis that she forgot the condoms she bought for this occasion. But thankfully, Michael remembered. He reached into the pocket of his jeans and pulled out his own condom. He rolled it on expertly and pushed Rosie gently onto the bed. Her body was amazing. Almost plump but not quite. Her breasts were full with dark brown areola and prominent nipples against her light brown skin. He sucked her breasts until she moaned. He opened her legs and kissed her inner thighs. She pulled on him urgently, ready to feel his dick inside of her. Understanding her cues, he lifted her hips and entered her. Even though she was wet and ready, the pain was sharp but strangely gratifying. She did not cry out, but she clung fiercely to him for a moment and then instinctively, she moved her body to his rhythm until he came and lay flat against her body. She could feel their juices flowing onto the sheets and she smiled to herself as she thought about having to pull the sheets off the bed she shared with her sister. She would have to take them to the laundromat in the morning.

"Are you okay?" he asked her, realizing the significance of the moment. "I wish you'd told me."

"I'm better than okay," she said and held onto him tightly. "I'm so happy."

Rosie and Michael spent virtually every day of the next month together. They went to the courthouse and got married 3 days before flying to Houston, Texas and starting their life together in a small apartment on Almeda Road. Now thirty years later, Michael Turner had built a tremendously successful architecture firm which had been featured in Black Enterprise Magazine. They had two children they adored, and a dream house designed by Michael. And today they would reaffirm their love before all their friends and family.

"So, Miss Rosie, you mean to tell me you married a man after knowing him for just one month?" Tawny sat back incredulous, laughing and waving a makeup brush. "Now that is some powerful mojo Mr. Turner put on you."

"Yes, I did, baby. And I have never had one moment of regret. You'll know when it's right for you. And always remember mojo works both ways." She winked, stood and removed the satin robe she was wearing and slipped into an elegant long sleeved white lace designer dress and white satin shoes with rhinestone detailing. She and her daughter walked together down a long hall to the top of the spiral staircase of Rosie and Michael's incredible 7000 square foot house, designed by Michael himself. Her son Brian was waiting for them. He took his mother's right arm and Ashley took the left. They descended the stairs together where Michael Turner waited for them at the altar decorated with pink and white roses.

Chapter 3

Ashley Turner was being honored by The Association of Rice University Black Alumni (ARUBA) for her accomplishments in the business world. Rice University is one of the premier colleges in the United States. Ashley graduated with a degree in Architecture and immediately joined her father's firm, MT Architecture, LP. She got her MBA from the University of Houston and quickly used her marketing skills to help the company skyrocket to one of the most successful minority owned architectural businesses in the country. The company was flourishing and had just been featured in Black Enterprise Magazine.

Ashley was driven and talented, but she knew how to have fun too. She accepted her award with grace at the podium and then took her seat next to her best friend and fellow Rice graduate, Kirk Ellison. Ashley and Kirk had been friends since they were high school freshmen.

"Great speech, Ash. Humble and lighthearted. Well done. You're getting really good at these things," Kirk said.

"Thanks. But does anybody really care? You know everybody just wants to visit the cash bar and wait for the DJ to start the party."

"Of course, but everybody is all decked out, so they want to be seen. And you need to be seen, girl. You look gorgeous as usual."

"Thanks, Kirk. You don't look so bad yourself."

Ashley was tall and lean, a gift from her father. He had given her the childhood nickname of "Slim." But she had grown out of awkward skinny lankiness and into slender elegance. She was medium brown skinned, the perfect artist's rendition of a combination of her mother's olive skin and her father's darkness. She had classically beautiful high cheekbones, sensuous full lips and big, long lashed eyes. She wore her hair very short eschewing the long weave trend and embracing the classic short do of 90's Halle Berry or Anita Baker or present-day Tamron Hall. Ashley Turner was a stunning woman who at 28 years still got stopped every so often by someone asking if she had ever considered modeling.

Tonight, Ashley wore a bright green satin one shoulder gown. The dress was very simple, almost a slip dress. Not many other women in the room could have pulled it off but it was perfect for Ashley. Tasteful and appropriate but still sexy.   Later when the party was finally rocking, Ashley found herself sitting at the table alone. Kirk, ever the gentleman, was dancing with another one of their old classmates. Ashley seized the moment to glance at her phone. No important messages or texts.

"Would you like to dance?" a voice from behind her inquired. She turned to see a hand extended attached to a very handsome, vaguely familiar man.

"Sure," she said as she rose from her seat. The song was a slower one, so the dance floor cleared out until there were just a few dancers on the floor.

"Have we met?" Ashley asked.

"No, we haven't and that makes me a little sad," the man said. "It's about time, don't you think?" He was smiling and looking down at Ashley which was rare because at 5'10 and wearing stilettos, she usually towered over the men who approached her.

"I'm Sebastian Campbell, I'm the new co-anchor on the morning news at Channel 11. Do you get up early? Maybe that's where you've seen me."

"Of course, it is. I guess I should stop channel surfing now that I've met you. I'm Ashley Turner, by the way."

"I know who you are Ashley. You are one of the illustrious honorees. You were right up there with the Astronaut and the Poet Laureate of Indiana. Very impressive bunch."

"I think you're making fun of me, but I forgive you." Ashley looked up at Sebastian. Their skin tones were very similar, caramel and smooth. His smile was wide and easily offered. His teeth glistening and white. No doubt a requirement for his job. He wore his thick hair closely cropped and he had a widow's peak. His eyes were a lighter shade of brown verging on hazel. Ashley thought for a minute that he might be too handsome, too ready for TV cookie cutter good looking, too perfect looking. The only thing that saved him from this fate was the slight gap between his two perfect front teeth. It gave him a boyish mischievous look and she liked that.

"How did you happen to come to this event? It's not exactly high profile."

"The station Community Affairs department bought two tickets and with me being the new guy in town and a person of color, they offered them to me. I thought it might be a good way to meet people. And I was right." He nodded slightly as he looked at her. "I'm glad I came."

"I am too," Ashley said. "I'm curious. Who did you give the other ticket to?"

His expression was sheepish. "I was stood up. One of my friends ditched me for a Rockets game." The song was ending but they stood on the floor for a beat assessing each other. As they were turning to walk back to their seats, Sebastian said "I'd like to see you again, Ashley."

"I'd like that too," she said. He pulled his cell phone out of his pocket and opened his contacts. "What's your number?" She gave it to him. "I feel bad for your date though. I guess this breaks the Bro rules, but as Hamilton says, 'I am not gonna miss my shot'."

"You're not stepping on anyone's toes, my date is a good friend, not a date date."

"Good to know. I'll talk to you soon."

Back at her seat, Kirk asked "Do you know that guy?"

"Not yet, but I think I'm going to get to know him," she said.

CHAPTER 4

The next morning Ashley watched Sebastian Campbell on the morning news. He was earnest and sincere during the news pieces and charming and quick witted during the lighthearted segments. She googled him and found out he had been a general assignments reporter and a weekend anchor for the CBS affiliate in Chicago before coming to Houston. Originally from Los Angeles, he graduated from UCLA and got his first TV job in San Diego before moving to Chicago. 34 years old. No wife. No children. Thank God for the internet. She would have to pretend surprise when they shared information about each other during the inevitable small talk.

Two days later, Sebastian arrived at Ashley's door to take her to dinner. He wore a khaki blazer, a crisp white shirt and pressed jeans. Ashley wore a simple sleeveless black linen dress with a prominent gold zipper in the back. She accessorized with striking gold earrings and bracelets. They were a beautiful couple. They sat in a back booth in Ashley's favorite sushi restaurant. Several people approached to ask for a selfie with Sebastian. He good naturedly agreed and chatted with a few others. He was accessible and easygoing.

"Do people recognize you everywhere you go?" Ashley asked. "That must get tiresome."

"Not yet, because it's new to me really. This is a much more high profile job than my Chicago gig. This was a big promotion for me. On air 5 days a week is a huge step up. I'll let you know when I grow tired of it." He leaned forward in the booth. "But enough about me. Tell me about your work."

"You probably heard more than you wanted to at the dinner the other night. But basically, we have a family business. My dad started the company and my mom helped him build the business. She kept the books, made sales calls, all the backend stuff while Dad did the designs and managed the projects. Now we all work in the business. I'm an architect, my brother is a landscape architect and Mom does interior design. But there would be no firm without my Daddy's vision and talent." Ashley sat straight up in her seat as she talked about the business.

"You have a lot to be proud of, Ashley. Generational wealth is rare in our community." He reached for her hand as he spoke, and Ashley felt a warmth pass between them that aroused her. She liked this man. They talked about everything under the sun. Politics, art, movies, the competitive news business, family.

"I love kids," Sebastian said. "I have three brothers. I know most men want sons, but I would love to have a daughter. Even two or three."

The waiter was hovering now, and they realized he probably wanted them to leave. They paid the bill and left agreeing they had to do this whole thing again soon.

At Ashley's door, they kissed deeply. Sebastian pulled her into his well-muscled arms. He ran his fingers along the zipper on the back of her dress, but he did not pull it. He savored the sweet smell of her that was vaguely fruity like cherries. She wrapped her arms around his neck and received the kisses he planted on her neck and shoulders.

The next time they saw each other was at a get together for Kirk's birthday. It was at Ashley's townhouse in Midtown. She was not fond of cooking and Kirk was vegan which was way beyond her culinary expertise. She had the food catered and served good wines and hard liquor for the group of about 20 people. Kirk came early and they listened to his latest selection modern blues artists that he loved, and the rest of their Kendrick Lamar obsessed friends tolerated. They shared a joint on the patio and just basked in the closeness they had nurtured for almost half their lives.

"So, we get to meet the celebrated Sebastian Campbell tonight. Up close and personal," Kirk said.

"I think you'll like him. He's down to earth. He doesn't send off any egotistical vibes. You know that's a turnoff for me."

"I'll give him the once over. Make sure he's good enough for you. You deserve the best." She reached over and took his hand. She squeezed it and brought it to her lips and kissed it.

"I don't know what I'd do without you, Kirk. Happy Birthday, love."

"I'll always be here for you, Ash. You can count on me. And thank you. Think about it. We are almost 30 years old."

"I know, right? And you are the only one who never ages. I hate you." She looked at her friend who didn't look much different than he had on his high school graduation day. He was average height with a trim compact body. He had the smooth brown skin of a teenager and had never shaved in his life. His was a sweet face that grandmothers would love to pinch. Both of his arms were tattooed sleeves which he kept covered with long sleeved shirts at the middle school where he taught math.

Ashley closed her eyes for a few minutes. She may have even dosed, unaware that Kirk never looked away from her. After a while, she roused herself.

"I'm going to change clothes," she said, pulling her hand away and kissing Kirk on the cheek as she rose.

Sebastian arrived fashionably late with a nice Prosecco and a bouquet of flowers.

"I love your place," he said admiring her collection of African art and abstract pieces in rich colors. "Nice to see you have not succumbed to the steel gray and silver trends. There's a lot of warmth in your place."

"Nice to see you noticed," she said.

Ashley introduced him to her friends. "Happy Birthday," he said to Kirk.

"Thanks, man. I'm glad you came by to help me celebrate."

"I hear you're a fan of Gary Clark Jr.," Sebastian said.

"I am indeed. Are you?"

"Definitely, what's the local blues scene like here?"

"I can recommend some spots. Let me know if you ever want to check it out. We can ditch Ashley. She doesn't get it." He winked at Ashley.

"I will for sure. Sounds like fun"

"And I will happily not join in," Ashley said.

Later as people were leaving, Kirk said to Ashley "I think Sebastian is cool. You could do worse."

"I have done worse," she said.

He hugged her and said, "Look, I'm gonna grab Linc and Shelley and head out. Give you some time to spend with Sebastian. I'll help you clean up first."

"You don't have to do that, honey. There's not much to do and tomorrow is Saturday. I have all day to clean. Happy Birthday, Kirk." They hugged goodbye.

Ashley closed the door behind the last person to leave. Sebastian approached her as she stood by the door. He moved very close to her. Her scent intrigued him.

"Great party," he said. He pulled her into an embrace kissing first her neck and then her lips. He nibbled her lips ever so lightly before inserting his tongue into her mouth. Ashley was wearing a long skirt wrapped around her body and secured with a tie at her waist. The fabric was thin. She could feel his firm erection against her legs as she grew wetter and wetter. Sebastian untied the string that secured her skirt and the skirt fell to the floor. They were still standing in the hallway. He removed her thong and she stepped out of it. He dropped to his knees and pulled her gently down onto the very expensive Oriental rug in the entry way. He lay on his back and pulled her hips over his mouth so he could eat her with abandon. She rose up and down on her knees screaming in ecstasy. When he brought to her climax, she grasped at his jeans and pulled them down. He was not wearing underwear. He slipped out of his jeans but not before reaching for a condom in his back pocket. Ashley took it from his hands and rolled it on to his enormous glistening dick with confidence. He pulled off his t-shirt revealing a toned and muscular, hairless chest the color of sweet butterscotch. Ashley pulled off her tank top and thin lacy bra revealing large, firm and beautiful breasts incongruous with her slender build. Sebastian pulled Ashley onto his perfectly shaped rock-hard dick as he sat on the floor. He sucked and bit gently on her breasts as she rode his dick and he thrusted in and out of her body until they both came in a tandem shutter. "Oh, my God," Ashley said as she finally rested in Sebastian's strong arms.

Ashley and Sebastian did not leave her house again until Sebastian left at nearly midnight on Sunday to go home and shower. Happily, exhausted, he cursed his 2:00 AM alarm but rose like a champion to make his 3:00 AM slot at the station.

Ashley turned on the TV just in time to see his gap-toothed smile and hear him say, "Good Morning Houston, I'm Sebastian Campbell."

CHAPTER 5

Ashley stood in the hot shower for a very long time thinking about her weekend with Sebastian. She had a rug burn on her knee and the makings of a bruise on her ass, but she did not care. She touched the spots tenderly and smiled remembering how she had earned these wounds. She stroked her sponge between her legs. The thoughts of Sebastian quickly moistened her pussy. She rubbed her fingers gently and rhythmically on her sweet spot until she shuddered in a Sebastian-inspired climax.

Later Ashley sat at her art deco-inspired desk in her office at MT Architecture, LP. Her father, Michael knocked on her door.

"Come on in," she called out.

"Hey Sweetheart, how was your weekend?" Michael entered holding a cup of coffee in one hand and a rolled up blueprint in the other. He was casually dressed in slacks and an Oxford shirt which meant he had no appointments for the day. Ashley had always thought of her father as the handsomest man she knew. She adored him. He was brilliant, funny, kind and generous. At

53, he was still lean but powerfully built, a testament to one hour each morning on his Peleton and 3 sessions each week with a personal trainer. His black hair and beard were lightly peppered with salt. Ashley did not think she was biased when she thought of him as the perfect man.

"Coffee? Black with one sugar."

"Thanks, Daddy. My weekend was great. I threw a little party for Kirk's birthday."

Michael sat in the chair across from Ashley's desk and slid the coffee across to her.

"When are you going to give Kirk a chance? He loves your dirty drawers. You know that don't you? And he's a good guy. Intelligent and respectful. I wouldn't mind him as a son-in-law."

Ashley rolled her eyes as she sipped her coffee. This was old territory for them.

"Daddy, it's never gonna happen. I love Kirk so much but not like that. I don't want to jeopardize our friendship. I feel like everything would change between us and I like it the way it is. Besides, we tried it once and we both got the giggles."

"Tried what? Now I don't know if I want to hear this."

"No, no, Daddy. We kissed. That's it. Nothing spicier than that. Besides I've met someone else, and I want to see where it goes."

"Who is it? Do I need to check him out?"

"It's way too early for that. This is not my prom date. You don't have to take pictures of us with our matching corsages. If it lasts beyond a few weeks, I'll introduce you."

Michael held up his hand and stood to leave the room.

"Okay, I'll wait. But just so you know if you're not married by the time you're 30, I am going to match you with Kirk like the Indian families do. I'll give his parents two goats and some chickens to take you."

"What?! The hell with that. I'm worth at least ten goats." She threw a pencil at him as he left.

CHAPTER 6

Sebastian was exhausted. He left the station and went directly home and slept for six hours. He would have to take an Ambien before bed to get himself back to his new sleep schedule. This early morning broadcast time was taking some getting used to. He rarely went to bed before midnight in Chicago. He had to admit he missed the city, his friends, the vibe. He missed it but Houston was growing on him, especially now that he had met Ashley Turner. He had approached her out of curiosity at first. Truthfully, his motives were not at all pure, but she was a knockout. She was bright, witty, interesting and sexy as hell. She had surprised him. She was special. He dared to think they could make it as a couple.

Four years before, Sebastian had gotten a freelance assignment to write an article for a black business journal on the arrival of the architect Michael Turner in Chicago. Michael had just opened his Chicago office and already he had won a commission to design a new building for a prominent nonprofit. Sebastian called Michael and they agreed to meet for dinner to discuss the article. Sebastian arrived early and sat at a table near the back of the restaurant where he could conduct the interview quietly. Sebastian was glued to his phone and did not notice Michael until he stood across from him at the table. He offered his hand and a breathtaking smile. He wore a dark, impeccably tailored suit. A Tag Heuer watch embraced his wrist. He wore no other jewelry other than his gold wedding band.

"I'm Michael Turner," he said. Sebastian stood and took his hand.

"Thank you for agreeing to the interview, Mr. Turner."

"I'm Sebastian Campbell."

"What are you drinking, Sebastian?"

"A Malbec. It's Argentine, not bad for the price." Michael motioned for the waiter. "Would you bring us a bottle of the Catena Zapata Argentino Malbec, please?"

"Of course, sir."

Sebastian had only to taste a sip of the Catena Zapata to know this wine was way over his budget. He watched Michael Turner carefully. He took charge of the evening brandishing his superior knowledge of food and wines. It was obvious he was a man used to being in command. When they finished the interview and the excellent bottle of wine, Sebastian reached for the check but Michael gently took it from his hands and pulled out his black American Express Card.

"You don't have to do that," Sebastian said. "I invited you to dinner. It's a business dinner. I can voucher it."

"Forget it," Michael said. "No sense trying to explain the wine. You may not want to voucher it. It's fine."

"Thank you. Thanks so much. I will let you know when the article comes out. You've been great. It will be flattering, I promise." His smile was wide and genuine.

"Which way are you going? Do you want to share an Uber?" Michael asked.

"Thanks for the offer but I'm not far from here. I could use the walk."

"Do you mind if I walk with you? Fresh air sounds good."

"Sure, I'm only two blocks away from here. You could call your Uber from there if you want to."

They stepped out into the brisk Chicago air. Sebastian pulled his wool scarf tighter around his neck. Michael seemed unfazed by the cold. He did not shudder or even slow the rate of his conversation. Their hands kept casually bumping as they walked. Neither of them felt compelled to allow more space between the two of them

"The temperature is dropping. Typical Chicago weather. It's cold as hell and you don't seem to mind it at all, man," Sebastian said.

"I'm originally from Syracuse, New York. This is not really cold. This is just a cool breeze to me."

"Well, I'm from LA. This is cold as fuck to me. After 3 years here, I still haven't gotten used to it." They walked in companiable silence until Sebastian stopped in front of a 3-story red brick building. "Well, this is me," he said. Michael looked intently at Sebastian, holding his gaze. He tilted his head slightly and gently pulled on Sebastian's scarf his fingers lingering on the wool.

"Would you like to come in?"

"Yes, I'd like that."

Michael followed Sebastian up to his second-floor apartment. The apartment was small but neat, a typical bachelor flat with empty glasses on the kitchen counter and a huge LED TV as the centerpiece.

"Have a seat. Would you like a beer?"

Michael did not sit. He did not accept the offer of beer. He faced Sebastian and took his face into his hands and kissed him. Sebastian returned the kiss. His body warmed. He could feel his dick growing hard. He felt Michael's erection pressed against him. He could feel the muscles of his chest underneath his expensive monogrammed shirt.

They undressed quickly with Michael's expensive designer clothes mingling on the floor with Sebastian's J Crew sweater and corduroy pants. Michael's body was impressive. Dark brown skin, muscled but not overly so. His dick approached ten inches when fully erect. The head glistened, waiting for Sebastian to take it into his mouth to taste that familiar salty sweet cum. Michael stood while Sebastian fell to his knees in front of him and sucked his dick and licked his balls. He groaned with pleasure as he held on to Sebastian's head and waited for his turn to return the favor.

His eyes closed, he whispered hoarsely "Let's get in bed." Sebastian led him into his messy room. The bed was unmade, the floor was cluttered. Sebastian reached into a bedside table and pulled out two rubbers and a tube of lubricant. He was in control now. The older, more successful man lay down on his back waiting. Sebastian lifted his legs up and spread the lube around Michael's waiting orifice. Then he plunged his hugely erect dick into Michael's ass. "Oh, yes. Yes, yes," Michael said. "Go deeper, please." Sebastian complied. Michael kept his eyes closed in his reverie. He repeated "Yes, yes" until Sebastian was spent and lay across his chest. His warm breath was comforting to Michael. Michael kissed the younger man and held him tightly, their legs intertwined.

Finally, Michael said "I really have to go but I want to see you again. I'll be at the Langham until Friday. Can you come by there?"

"Yes," Sebastian said.

"I better get going. I have an early morning." Michael stood and went into the living room to retrieve his clothes. Sebastian followed him without bothering to dress. In the open living area, Sebastian stopped at the refrigerator to get a bottle of water. Michael watched Sebastian as he was pulling on his clothes. The sight of Sebastian took his breath away. His torso was long and his even the skin on his back was perfectly unblemished. He was broad shouldered with a rippled abdomen, narrow hips and long legs that made Michael think of an Olympic long jumper. His ass was round and inviting to Michael. He imagined spreading the cheeks and fucking him but that would have to wait. Fully dressed, he pulled out his phone and dialed Uber.

"My car will be here in 9 minutes," he said. "I'll go on downstairs."

Sebastian walked over to him and kissed him deeply, his erection rising again. He would deal with that on his own later.

"I'll see you at the Langham tomorrow. Or tonight, really. It's 2AM," he said.

Michael could not stop thinking about Sebastian. He was distracted at work the next day watching the clock like a college kid working in the mailroom. The Chicago office was small. There were two architects and an office manager on the staff. Everyone was shocked when he left work at 5PM. He usually closed the office in the evening long after the staff had gone home.

Later he sat in his luxurious room at the Langham drinking a cognac. It was 7PM. His phone vibrated with a text from Sebastian. **Be there in 30.** He texted back. **I'll order room service.**

Sebastian was not the first man Michael had slept with. He had fucked men in New York City, Miami, and LA but never in Houston. He believed in that adage that you don't shit where you eat. He was always discreet. Always circumspect. He never saw the same man more than two or three times. But Sebastian was different. There was something about him that drew him in. He could not get him out of his mind. He would find that he needed to see him. Sebastian would be the first man he would fall in love with.

Friday morning at the Langham hotel, Michael and Sebastian stood in a hot shower together their lean bodies entwined under the steamy water.

"When are you coming back?" Sebastian asked.

"In about a month," Michael said. "Maybe I can stay through a weekend next time."

"That would be awesome."

They got out of the shower and dried each other's bodies. When they were dressed, Michael walked Sebastian to the door. He picked up his wallet from the coffee table. He pulled out 5 crisp $100 bills and handed them to Sebastian. Sebastian pushed his hand away.

"Listen to me," he said. "I don't want your money. Being with you makes me feel good. When it stops feeling good, I'm out. Do you understand?"

"I understand." They kissed like they might never have the chance to kiss again, and Michael closed the door behind him.

Chapter 7

Michael Turner was the only child of a couple who married late in life and did not become parents until they were in their forties. His father worked as a baggage handler at the Syracuse airport. His mother operated a beauty shop in the basement of their home. Michael was a bookish, introverted child, a straight A student, an Eagle Scout and active member of the United Methodist youth group. He was not athletic and preferred building model airplanes to playing sports. The Turners adored their boy. He was also incredibly handsome and was 6'2" tall by the time he was 16.

When Michael was 17, he lay in his bed reading a Stephen King novel when someone knocked on his door. "Come in," he said. Ettalyn Burke, one of his mother's clients, entered the room. She was 22 years old, pretty in the manner of neighborhood girls, slightly overweight. "Hey Mike, what you are doing?" Michael looked behind the woman expecting to see his mother. She was not there.

"Nothing. Just reading a book." Ettalyn moved closer to him, climbing into bed with him. Michael stiffened. He was at a loss for words. Ettalyn took the book out of his hands and lay it on the floor next to the bed. She pulled up her dress and climbed on top of Michael. She was not wearing underwear.

"Would you like to fuck me?" She did not wait for an answer. She unzipped his pants and pulled them down. He had the beginnings of an erection. She leaned down and sucked his dick until he was rock hard. Michael was breathing heavily but he did not know what to do. He had never had sex before. Ettalyn straddled him, pulling her skirt up around her waist. She closed her eyes and raised up and down fiercely until she came, and he did too, his juices spirting wildly.

"Was this your first time, baby?" His eyes were closed, his hands covering his mouth. He nodded.

"Well next time you have to move more. You can't just lay there." she said. "I'll show you what to do." She kissed him and patted his cheek then moved off him, pulled her skirt down. She glanced in the mirror above the dresser fluffing her curls out with her long red nails.

"Next time I'll come before your mama does my hair," she said.

"See you, Mike," she said as she waved goodbye and closed the door behind her. Michael stood up surveying the stickiness of his penis and balls. He touched himself gingerly and stood up and stripped completely naked. There was a wet spot on the bottom sheet of his bed. He pulled the sheet off the bed and bundled it with his jeans and t-shirt and threw everything into the dirty clothes hamper in his closet. Then he walked down the hall to bathroom and took a near scalding shower.

Ettalyn would come to Michael's room many times over the next year.

"Get on top. Move up and down. Suck my titties. You can bite them a little bit. Not too hard. Kiss me. Use your tongue more."

Ettalyn instructed and Michael's instincts took over where her lessons left off. By the time he left for Columbia University a year later, he was an experienced lover. He knew what he was supposed to do and where he was supposed to suck or touch but he found no real pleasure in it. He'd assumed he would be constantly aroused now that he was fucking but he wasn't. He truly didn't get what all the fuss was about.

He and Ettalyn did not talk. He wondered why she chose him when there were a lot of single men in the neighborhood. She marveled at all the books in his room.

"Do you like to do anything else but read?" she asked him once, but she did not wait for the answer. She looked out the window to make sure the coast was clear and made her way outside. Michael watched as she hurried down the sidewalk toward her house. It would not be until years later in a Human Sexuality class at Columbia University that Michael would come to understand that Ettalyn Burke had sexually assaulted him.

CHAPTER 8

Michael Turner was a brilliant student at Columbia. By the time he met Rosalinda Olivares on the train, he was no longer the shy boy from Syracuse. He was smart, ambitious, and determined. He could look in the mirror, so he knew his good looks were an asset. He was confident his future would be bright. He dreamed of the picture-perfect life with a beautiful wife and 2 or 3 children. He dated beautiful, intelligent and aspiring women at Columbia. The sex was good, and the women were receptive. And every night he prayed that his desire and longing to have sex with men would go away.

Three months before Michael married Rosalinda, he made plans to meet a friend at a gallery in Harlem. His friend was held up at work and had to cancel, so he went alone. He walked through the gallery admiring the pieces. When he stopped at a particularly interesting black and white drawing of an old woman, a man approached him.

"What do you think of this one?" the man asked.

"I think it's amazing. I like it a lot," Michael said.

"Thank you," the man said. Michael looked at the man standing next to him. He was a slight man with olive skin and a magnificent head of black curls. His eyes were a stunning shade of green that could have been contact lenses, but they were too clear and piercing not to be real. Michael guessed him to be around 40 years old.

"So, you must be Diego Rodriquez Mata," Michael said.

"I am indeed," Diego said offering his hand. Michael shook Diego's hand and held it for a beat longer than expected.

"And what is your name?"

"My name is Michael Turner." Diego looked at Michael with those catlike eyes and Michael felt a shudder run the length of his spine.

"May I buy you a coffee, Michael?" Diego asked. Michael and Diego left the gallery and headed for a coffee shop where they ordered black coffees and cake.

"I am in town for a few months for the gallery show and to lecture at NYU. I am from Argentina."

"Have you been here before?" Michael asked.

"This is my third time. And the third time is the charm. Isn't that what you Americans say? This time I have met you, my friend." Diego leaned forward in his seat with his hands clasped under his chin. Michael was entranced by the straightforward way Diego looked at him. He could feel warmth in the center of his body. "Let's go to my place," he said. Michael's apartment was a third-floor walkup, one room with a futon. It was paid for with scholarship and grant money.

They were barely inside the door when they undressed and fell on to the futon. Diego was a small wiry man with thick black hair on his chest and abdomen. He was agile and aggressive like a small terrier. There was no question of who was in charge. Michael was shocked at the size of his dick. For a small man it was quite impressive, uncircumcised and hard as granite. Michael took it into his mouth and sucked fiercely until Diego released his juices in spasmodic rhapsody. When he saw Michael's erection, he unselfishly returned the favor. He sucked Michael's dick expertly and tenderly suckled his balls. When Michael seemed on the verge of coming, he positioned himself on all fours in front of him. Michael needed no other prompting, he spat on his fingers and moistened Diego's asshole before he plunged his huge dick inside. The smaller man roared with pleasure. "Esta bien rico! Si, si, si !" he screamed. When Michael came, they fell into a clump on the small futon but Diego was not a selfish lover. He pushed Michael onto his back while raising his legs up over his slender shoulders. He used his tongue to moisten Michael's waiting ass thrusting in until Michael lost track of all time and place.

Michael and Diego would spend the next three months enjoying New York City and fucking. Diego was staying at a very nice apartment near NYU. He was from a wealthy Argentine family so money was no object. They did not look beyond the time they spent together. There was no future for them. Diego was married and had three children. His wife and children were beautiful. Diego proudly shared photos of his family. They lived in Buenos Aires in a lovely home with a garden. Diego already had the life Michael wanted so much.

"You can have it all too, mi amigo," Diego said. "But you must find a proper wife. It is my belief that you must find a wife who not only loves you but who loves what you can provide as well. Material things are not everything, but they are very important for a happy wife. And the woman should not be too ambitious. If she is ambitious, she may grow bored with her life as a wife. Such a woman will expect more from you. Your wife should always be grateful for everything you provide. I hope you find this sort of woman, Miguel. If you do, you will have an amazing life."

Two weeks after Diego flew back to Argentina, Michael Turner met Rosalinda Olivares on the subway and soon he knew he had found his perfect wife.

CHAPTER 9

Ashley and Sebastian lay in bed enjoying the sound of rain outside. Sebastian was still slipping in and out of sleep while she watched the CBS Morning News. "This is good sleeping weather" her mother would say. It was Sunday too so they could luxuriate in the simple act of doing nothing. Ashley thought about how easygoing Sebastian was. He didn't resent her for the long hours she worked. He fit in with her friends. He had introduced her to the friends he'd made since he got to Houston. They liked the same kinds of movies. They cooked together. And the sex was amazing too. They had been dating for two months. Ashley weighed in her mind whether it was time to introduce him to her family. Her mother was planning a party to celebrate her brother getting his master's degree. She thought that might me a good time to do it. But for now, she just turned off the TV and fell into a comfortable sleep with Sebastian. The buzzing of her cellphone woke her up. It was her mother.

"Don't tell me you're still in bed. It's almost 10 o'clock. I've already been to mass."

"Yes, I am still in bed."

"Alone?" Ashley rolled her eyes and stretched like a languid cat next to Sebastian. Sebastian stirred and wrapped his arms around her rubbing his erection against her thigh. Ashley did not answer her mother's question.

"So, when do we get to meet this mystery man?" Rosalinda asked. "We almost never get to see you anymore. I miss you."

"I see Daddy every day, Mom," Ashley said.

"But you don't see me every day and I am the nosy one. This new guy must be pretty special. Why don't I just make dinner for you two? A nice Dominican meal and the coconut pie you like. What do you think?"

"That sounds good. How about Saturday? I'll bring a bottle of that tropical blend wine you like."

"Okay, baby. I'll see you Saturday." Ashley laid her phone on the nightstand. Then she wrapped her long legs around Sebastian as he slipped the shiny tip of his dick into her wet pussy. When the full length of it was inside of her, they moved together in that timeless way to which they had so quickly grown accustomed.

CHAPTER 10

Ashley was born exactly one year to the day her parents moved to Texas from New York. The newlyweds settled into a small one-bedroom apartment which was quite nice, based on New York standards. They bought a well-worn, 1980 Chevy Camaro. Like a lot of New Yorkers, Rosalinda had never been behind the wheel of a car, but she easily learned to drive. Michael enrolled in grad school at Rice and Rosalinda got a job as a directory assistance operator for Southwestern Bell. Michael worked part time as a draftsman for a construction company. Their low incomes went so much further in Houston than they would have in New York City. They were very happy.

Rosalinda was shocked when she found out she was pregnant. She was a good Catholic girl who confessed the sin of premarital sex to her parish priest and practiced the rhythm method. She charted her periods on an Allstate insurance company calendar she had taped on the door of her bedroom closet. She and Michael were careful not to have sex on the unsafe days but honestly even excluding the birth control method, they did not have sex as frequently as she wanted to. She would have been happy to fuck every night, but Michael seemed perfectly satisfied with once or twice a week.

Rosalinda flipped through the pages of the bestselling book, **The Joy of Sex.** She read the book from cover to cover and discreetly bought pornographic magazines. She had been married for three months and on this night, she was determined to ignite a flame of passion with her husband. She was not an experienced lover, but she knew enough to know that something was missing in her love life with Michael. She believed she was doing something wrong.

She looked at her naked reflection in the mirror. She saw a full breasted light brown skinned woman with rounded hips and curly black hair between her legs. She had the iconic hourglass figure that other women longed for. Her legs were shapely, and more than one man had complimented her on the allure of her feet and ankles. Her face was lovely and unblemished. Her hair thick and healthy looking. She felt pretty and tonight she wanted her husband to make her feel even prettier. She pulled on the black lace thong and matching bra that had cost her a whole day's pay. She sprayed Joy perfume behind her ears and on her neck. Then she lay on the bed and waited for Michael. When she heard his key in the door, she walked into the living room to greet him.

Michael released a slight gasp when he saw her "My God, you look like a goddess, Rosie. Incredible. Just incredible." He took her into his arms. "You smell good too."

"Come to bed with me," she said. She took him into the bedroom where she undressed him. She pulled his polo shirt over his head and unzipped his pants pulling them down. She was pleased to see the bulging in his crotch. Michael stepped out of his pants and underwear. He unsnapped Rosalinda's bra and pulled the thong down around her ankles. She stepped out of it and drew him into bed with her. Seeing his beautiful body, she knew she could never grow tired of it. The sleek dark brown skinned contrasted against hers was such a powerful turn on to her. She could already feel her wetness flowing down her inner thigh. Michael could feel it too and he slipped his fingers into her body first. When he slid them out, he put them into his mouth to taste her. He pulled her to the edge of the bed and got down on his knees before her where he feasted on her pussy. His tongue seemed to have no limits to where it could reach. Rosalinda screamed "Oh my God, yes, yes. That feels so, so good."

Her legs were wrapped around his head and shoulders and still he continued until she yelled, "Fuck me now. Please fuck me now." Michael raised himself up and complied, plunging his huge dick into her pussy thrusting and arching his back as he did so. The force was so full and strong that it was almost painful, but Rosalinda did not mind. The pain made her feel alive. The pain reminded her that Michael desired her. She shuddered uncontrollably when she reached her climax and Michael responded in kind. He spilled his juices with a force and magnitude that left them wet and exhausted.

Later Rosalinda and Michael would calculate that this was the night their beloved daughter Ashley was conceived. Privately, they would call her the "black lace thong baby." Two years later, Brian was born. Their perfect family was complete.

CHAPTER 11

Sebastian Campbell was the son of two high school teachers in Los Angeles. His mother was an unbelievably beautiful woman who had once been a professional jazz singer. His father worked two jobs to support his wife and four young boys. Camille Campbell died when Sebastian was 16. Sebastian was the oldest of the brothers. A popular, straight A student and one of the top high school hurdlers in California, he turned down a scholarship to Harvard to stay in LA to be there for his family.

One morning, Sebastian's little brother, Marcus, shook him. He was in a deep sleep and did not grasp what was happening at first. Sebastian's middle name is Joseph and close family and friends called him Joey as a boy.

"Joey," the little boy said. "Mom won't wake up." He stood staring at Sebastian, unblinking. "She was supposed to take us to baseball practice today. She's still sleeping." Sebastian roused himself enough to grasp what the 8-year-old was saying. He sat up in his bed rubbing his eyes. It was a Saturday morning, and his plans did not include getting up at 8:00 am. His brother Daniel was snoring in the bunkbed above him.

"Go put your clothes on. I'll take you to practice. I'll wake Mom up first. She's just real tired." Marcus left the room to change clothes. Sebastian's father was gone to his second job as a hotel front desk clerk. His mother was no doubt exhausted. She taught school, gave private voice lessons and took care of all of them. He would drive his little brothers to practice and then come back and make breakfast for her.

Sebastian looked into his parents' bedroom. He sensed something amiss the moment he walked in the room. His mother lay flat on her back. Her head was turned away from him. There was vomit on her face and neck. Her eyes partially open. He lowered his head close to her face. He did not feel breath.

"Mom, Mom, mom," he screamed as he shook her. She did not respond. She felt cold and clammy. He took her into his arms and tried to force her awake. He slapped her face. He shook her again harder. He squeezed her so hard he feared her might break her ribs. The other boys, Marcus, Daniel and Drew came running in.

"What's the matter with Mom? What is it?" Daniel yelled. He stood at the door unable to enter the room.

"Call 911, call 911" he yelled. Mobilized, Daniel ran to use the kitchen phone.

The two younger boys started to cry. They stood just inside the bedroom door.

"Wake up Mommy. Wake up. Wake up." Drew wailed. The little boy ran to his mother, climbed onto the bed and buried his face in his mother's bosom, his small body wracked with tears. She did not stir.

Camille Campbell had suffered a brain aneurysm and died moments after her husband kissed her goodbye and went to work.

Later, Sebastian's father Paul would say "The doctor says she didn't suffer. It happened quickly." But Sebastian would read about aneurysms later and find that she probably had an unbearable headache. She did indeed suffer if only for a moment. He would have nightmares about her suffering for the rest of his life and blame himself for not finding her sooner. He always believed he could have saved her.

Losing his mother, changed Joey Campbell's life completely. His father quit his parttime job so he could spend more time at home with his sons. His Aunt Lucy retired from the US Army after 32 years and moved in with the family. Joey became more focused on his studies. He won a track scholarship to UCLA. He worked part time at a grocery store. He helped his little brothers with their homework. His face grew solemn and serious way beyond his years.

His father straightened his tie as Sebastian pulled on his gown before his high school graduation ceremony.

"I am such a lucky man," Paul said. "I don't know what I did to deserve such an amazing son. I am so proud of you." His eyes filled with tears. He embraced his son. "I love you, son."

"I love you too, Dad." At 18, Sebastian was now much taller than his father. He kissed his father on the forehead. "I had the best role model in the world."

"Then I need you to do something for me, Joey."

"What? Anything you say, Daddy. What do you need?"

"I need you to be a kid again. I need you to laugh more and find some joy. Be a fuck up like every other 18-year-old boy. Let me and Lucy take care of your brothers. We got this. Have some fun, son. You deserve it." He stepped back from his son grasping his shoulders and smiling widely. "Promise me, boy."

"I promise."

Chapter 12

Sebastian and his long-term girlfriend broke up when he was junior at UCLA. They had dated since they were juniors in high school. They met on the track circuit, and both ended up at UCLA. Tasha Dailey was a world class 800-meter runner. She dropped out of school and went pro at the end of her sophomore year. The breakup was amicable, and they still talked and texted a few times a month. And occasionally when she was in town, they fucked. Tasha was doing well, and she even got a Nike endorsement deal. He'd heard she was dating Niles Allred, the retired Jamaican Olympic gold medal sprinter. He was now an ESPN analyst.

Sebastian's cell phone vibrated. It was Tasha. Her photo flashed on the screen. She was tall and slender with shapely and toned runner's legs. Her face was gorgeous, heart shaped with a sprinkling of brown freckles across her light brown face. She wore trademark long blonde braids which flew behind her like ribbons when she ran down the track.

"Hey, Tash. What's up?"

"Hey, you. How are you?"

"Doing great, nothing to complain about."

"Look, do you have plans for tomorrow night? I want you to meet Niles. Do you think the little brothers might get a kick out of it? We could come by your dad's house."

"Are you kidding me? They are all gonna shit bricks. Even Daddy and Auntie would be happy."

"Great! But tell Ms. Lucy not to cook anything. We'll order food. Niles will treat."

"Sounds great. See you around 7."

"We'll be there."

The younger boys could barely contain themselves when their father opened the door and Tasha walked in with Niles Allred. He was very tall, as dark as midnight and incredibly handsome. He did not wear a track suit or blue jeans. He wore pressed navy blue slacks and a light blue button down shirt. He carried a bouquet of flowers which he handed to Aunt Lucy.

"Thank you for inviting us into your home," he said in his distinctive Jamaican accent. Tasha hugged everyone in the family and handed Paul a bottle of Crown Royal.

"Don't think for a minute we forgot you, Mr. Campbell."

After a meal of catered Caribbean dishes and lots of laughs and reminiscing, Tasha said, "We should probably get going, we don't want to keep you guys up late too."

"There's no school tomorrow," Drew said.

"There's no need to rush," Aunt Lucy said. "Please stay."

"We really do have to go," Niles said. "But may we come back another time?"

"Yes, of course," Paul said.

"I can walk you out," Sebastian said.

"We were hoping you could come back to the hotel with us for a little while. We have some people we want you to meet," Tasha said. "We can drop you off at your apartment or bring you back here to get your car."

"We drove over together," Daniel said. "We're roommates again. I'll see you when I see you, bro. Have fun." He looked at the three of them with puppy dog eyes, hoping to angle an invitation to join them. It did not come.

Sebastian sat in the backseat of Niles' dark blue Tesla as they drove to the Ritz Carlton. As they were driving, Tasha turned in her seat on the front passenger side. Niles drove and was very quiet, but Sebastian could sense that he was looking at him in the rearview mirror.

"We want to have sex with you tonight, Joey. What would you think about that?" She stared at him directly waiting for him to respond. At the same time, she squeezed Niles' knee.

"What? What are you saying?" His mouth remained open after he spoke. "Is this a joke?"

Niles said "It's not a joke but you can say no. We don't want to pressure you." Sebastian could see Niles' face reflected in the mirror. "But Tasha wants me to fuck her, and I want you to fuck me. And later you can fuck her if you like. Maybe I'll watch.

Where is the harm? You might actually have some fun, no? We will go with the proverbial flow, yes?"

Sebastian looked first at Niles and then at Tasha. He expected her to laugh or tell him this was all a prank. But Tasha's face was earnest, her smile genuine.

Sebastian considered what they were proposing and said, "Why not?"

They were in the Executive Suite of the Ritz Carlton. Sebastian thought the room was probably bigger than his father's house. It had a full living and dining area and two bedrooms. The carpet was deep and plush. The rooms were decorated in tasteful shades of white, ecru, and taupe.

They had only been in the room for a few seconds when Tasha approached Sebastian and kissed him deeply. Her tongue explored his mouth in a way that was familiar to him. She pulled his Henley shirt out of his pants and over his head. Then she unzipped his pants and pulled down his briefs releasing his pounding erection. She undressed quickly and went into one of the bedrooms. Niles had also undressed. Sebastian could see that his body was magnificent. Sleek. Black. Not one pimple or mole. His ass was solid and rounded from years of athletic training. Sebastian's dick was pulsing. He could not tell if it was the site of Niles perfect body or Tasha's that had him reeling. Sensing his wonder at his situation, Niles came up to him and kissed him so passionately it left him shuddering. Niles' erection was unbelievably huge. Black as night and uncircumcised. Tasha reached into a drawer next to the bed. She handed each of the men a condom. She held a tube of lubricant in her hand. She stood behind Niles and spread the lubricant on her fingers and then in his asshole as he continued to kiss Sebastian.

She whispered hoarsely "Come to bed." She lay on the bed spreading her legs waiting while both men secured the condoms on their throbbing erections. Niles leaned over her and then entered her. As he did, he slid a pillow under her hips lifting her higher. Sebastian was paralyzed for a moment but then he took his cue from Niles' rising ass. He climbed into the bed on his knees and slid his penis into Niles' ass. It was a dryer, tighter feeling than a pussy. It was a different feeling but a very good feeling. Niles tightened his sphincter muscles around his dick, and he thought it felt amazing. Just as Niles was moaning and Tasha was too, Sebastian believed he could grow to like this feeling a lot. After they all came, each in their own time, they lay on the bed together drenched in sweat, the spent condoms were discarded somewhere in the bed. Three sets of the impossibly long legs of three physically gifted people linked together like pieces of a puzzle.

"So good. So good," Niles repeated. "Somehow I knew the minute I saw you it would be this good."

"I told you," Tasha said. "I knew you wouldn't be disappointed. I had a feeling it would be good for you too, Joey. Was it?"

"Incredible," he said. Tasha then leaned in to kiss Sebastian on the lips as Niles kissed her on the back of her neck.

Sebastian, Tasha and Niles would be together many more times over the course of the next few years. They would remain friends for the rest of their lives. They would end their physical relationship only after Niles and Tasha married and even then, not until she became pregnant with their first child. Sebastian was the little girl's godfather.

When Sebastian graduated from UCLA with a degree in Marketing, Niles helped him get a job with a local TV station in San Diego as a production assistant. His good looks, charm and hustle got him the chance to do an audition tape for a reporting job. He aced his audition and landed a spot as a general assignments reporter. He was a natural. He was engaging, hardworking and had a face the camera loved. He worked in the San Diego market until he got the weekend anchor job in Chicago where he met Michael Turner.

CHAPTER 13

The year before he moved to Houston, Sebastian sat in this stunning condo on Lake Shore Dr. He had spent every penny he had for the down payment, but the investment was already paying off. The apartment had already appreciated by 30%. He had Michael Turner to thank for his good investment advice and a gift of $25,000. Tonight, he would pay Michael back. He looked out of his window from the sixth floor and saw Michael get out of his Uber. He was impeccably dressed as always. He wore a camel-colored cashmere sweater and navy blue slacks with Zegna Italian loafers. His hair and beard were trimmed flawlessly. Sebastian watched him and waited for him to ring the bell.

The month before Sebastian had hosted his brother Daniel and his sister-in-law Jennifer for a week. They had a blast. Daniel and Jenn were happy and fun and now they were talking about starting a family.

"I know people hate it when family members ask these kinds of questions, but I'm going to risk it because I love you, Joey. Do you see yourself getting married?"

"Jenn, please," Daniel said.

"It's okay, Sis," Sebastian said. "If I meet the right woman, I am ready. You guys are lucky. You really are. I would love to get married and have a bunch of children."

Jennifer and Daniel were a cute couple. Jennifer was a petite brown skinned woman with enormous eyes and short natural hair. Daniel was a good-looking, shorter more compact version of his brother. They were both registered nurses in LA. They were perfect together and Sebastian was envious. He wanted what they had.

Sebastian heard the doorbell ring and he buzzed Michael in. They had a routine whenever he was in town. They would order food in and watch Netflix and then spend the rest of the night in bed. Tonight, Sebastian wanted to talk.

He opened the door and Michael entered smiling. Sebastian did not feel the familiar stirring when he saw him. He felt resolved. He closed the door and Michael pulled him into a kiss. Michael's body radiated in heat as it always did whenever he saw Sebastian. He circled his arms around his waist and said "I've missed you so much. It gets harder being away from you. I think about you all the time. I love you, Sebastian." He slipped his hand into the waistband of Sebastian's jeans and was surprised that he did not feel that familiar hardness.

"Is something the matter?" he asked. He stepped back and looked Sebastian squarely in the face. Sebastian closed his eyes, unable to look directly at him.

"I have something I need to talk to you about. Let's sit down for a minute." He took Michael's hand and let him to the couch. They sat and Sebastian reached into a tiny wooden box on the coffee table. He pulled out the certified check for $25,000 made out to Michael Turner. He handed Michael the check and said "I'm so grateful for everything you've done for me, Mike. You came into my life at just the right time. I love you, but we have to end this now." Michael's face went slack except for his eyes which widened with shock.

"Why? What's going on. Why now?" He dropped the check on the table and reached for Sebastian's hands. "Tell me. Have you met somebody else? What is it?"

"No, I haven't met anybody else, but I want to. And I just feel like this..." he pointed to Michael and back at himself. "This isn't helping. I want to focus on finding someone to love and who will love me. I'm tired of being a chapter of someone else's story. I want my own story."

"What do you mean 'your own story'? I am not deaf or blind. I hear things. I know things. I know you've fucked your share of women... and men in Chicago. What's kept you from settling down with one of them before? Do you even have it in you to be monogamous?" Michael wiped tears from his eyes.

"Maybe not, but I want to try. I want what you have. Are you going to tell me you never fuck Rosalinda? I wouldn't believe you.

You're selfish, Michael. You want everything including me, but you don't want me to have a wife and family like you have. That's not fair, is it?" He tried to hug Michael, but he pulled away from him angrily.

"So, who is there left for you to run after in Chicago? You think I don't know what you do?" he asked.

"Chicago is a big city, Michael. I'll take my chances. But my agent is looking at some other opportunities for me. I'm not bound to Chicago. I'll go where my career takes me. I kind of like the idea of a fresh start. There is nothing binding me to Chicago." He picked up the check from the floor and handed to Michael again. Michael took the check and stared at it for a long time before he stood up and slid it into the pocket of his pants. Sebastian stood too and took Michael into his arms and kissed him for the last time. Michael turned away from him and headed to the door.

He turned to Sebastian and said "Just so you know, Sebastian. I do love my wife. I love her dearly, but I have never loved anyone as much as I love you. I hope you change your mind about this. I really do. If you call me, I'll come back." He opened the door, stepped into the hall and closed the door behind him.

CHAPTER 14

Rosalinda opened the door of her sumptuous home to find her daughter standing with Sebastian Campbell. They were holding hands and smiling widely.

"Oh, my God. Come in. I know you," she said. "You're on the morning news."

"Mom, this is Sebastian Campbell," Ashley said as they stepped into the foyer. She hugged her mother tightly.

"It's a pleasure to meet you, Mrs. Turner." He extended his hand to shake but Rosalinda pulled him into a bear hug instead.

"We are huggers in this house," she said. "Come in and sit down." She led them into the elegant living room decorated with contemporary African American art which shared space with a sprinkling of earth toned abstracts. There were family portraits on a built-in bookshelf. Sebastian saw photos of the family collectively and individual photos of the parents and children. He was especially struck by a particular photo of Ashley and her parents. She was wearing her high school graduation cap and gown. Ashley and her mother faced the camera smiling, but

Michael Turner was staring at this daughter with unconcealed pride, a slight grin turning up the corner of his mouth.

"Where's Daddy?" Ashley asked.

"I forgot the whipped cream for the pie. He went to the store. He'll be right back."

Ashley and Sebastian took a seat on the plush couch with their backs to the kitchen. Rosalinda sat on a chair opposite them.

"Everything smells delicious, Mrs. Turner," Sebastian said.

"I hope you like Dominican food, Sebastian. We use a lot of rice and beans, plantains. There's some middle Eastern influence too."

"It sounds great," he said.

"Now, please tell me how you two met. I can't wait to hear about it."

Rosalinda looked behind them. She heard Michael open and close the refrigerator door.

"Here comes your father now. You can tell us both the story."

Ashley and Sebastian turned in their seats just as Michael walked in. Sebastian stood up and turned around. He offered his outstretched hand. Ashley turned around in her seat. Michael stood in the doorway, momentarily unable to move or speak. His knees weakened slightly. Acid rose in his throat. His ears throbbed.

Ashley stood and walked around to take her father's arm. Oblivious to his reaction, she took his hand and led him into the living room.

"Daddy, this is Sebastian Campbell. Sebastian, this is my father."

"I'm happy to finally meet you, sir," Sebastian said. He nodded slightly at Michael.

"It's nice to meet you too," Michael said. He shook Sebastian's hand. He kissed his daughter on the cheek and then sat unsteadily in the chair next to Rosalinda.

"This occasion calls for a drink," Rosalinda said "What is your pleasure, Sebastian? Would you like wine or beer or a cocktail? I've been making mojitos of late, and I think they are pretty good."

"I would love a mojito," he said.

"Wonderful, come help me in the kitchen, Ashley. Dinner will be ready soon. Give me another 15 minutes or so." She rose and Ashley followed her to the kitchen.

Michael leaned forward in his chair. "What the fuck are you doing here?" he whispered harshly. "What are you doing with my daughter? Did you come here looking for her?"

"It didn't happen like that, Michael. I did not seek her out. And I like Ashley a lot."

"Well, I don't give a fuck. When you leave here today, you need to get the hell away from her, do you understand me? Stay away from my daughter," he hissed.

Sebastian leaned forward this time, uncrossing his long legs and speaking directly to Michael but in a low voice. "I'm in love with Ashley and I am not going anywhere. I'm sorry if it hurts you but you need to get used to it."

"Your mojitos are ready," Rosalinda called from the kitchen. "Come and get em."

Sebastian rose and followed her voice to the kitchen. Michael stood and braced himself before following behind him. His knees felt like jelly. He thought he might have to sit back down again but he powered on.

Later after Ashley and Sebastian left, Rosalinda said "Michael, you were so rude to Sebastian. I have never seen you behave that way. What in heaven's name was wrong with you? It was embarrassing and I know Ashley was hurt by it."

"I don't like the guy. He's not right for Ashley."

"How do you know that? You didn't give the man a chance. When you weren't giving him the third degree, you were staring him down. He didn't deserve any of that. I thought he was lovely and it's obvious Ashley really likes him. What are you seeing that I didn't see?"

Michael walked to the home bar and poured two fingers of Glenfiddich Scotch into a glass. Rosalinda stood across from him, but he did not look up at her.

"Let's just chalk it up to a father's intuition. My gut tells me he is wrong for Ashley." He then drank the liquor in one swallow.

Ashley and Sebastian drove back to her place after dinner. They sat in silence for a few minutes before she spoke.

"Something strange was going on with my father tonight. I can't explain it. He wasn't very nice to you tonight. I'm sorry, Sebastian. He wasn't himself. He's usually the life of every party."

"Don't worry about it, Ash. Fathers can get a little bent out of shape when they get competition for their daughter's affection. Especially if it looks serious."

"Is this serious?"

"I think it is." He reached for her hand and held it to his lips and kissed it. "What do you think?"

"I think so too."

Ashley walked into her father's office on Monday morning and closed the door behind her. Her father was as handsome as ever behind his massive desk, but he seemed smaller, diminished, withdrawn. He appeared older. Ashley sat in the chair across from him. She perched on the edge of her seat.

"Daddy, can we talk about what happened Saturday night? Why were you so rude to Sebastian?"

"I don't think I was rude. I was wary."

"I beg to differ; you were flat out rude. But wary of what? You just met him. What is there to be wary of?"

"Have you forgotten I've worked in Chicago off and on for the last five years? I know a thing or two about Sebastian Campbell. Chicago is a small, big city for black folks, sweetheart."

"Then tell me what you know. If it's something that will hurt me, then shouldn't you tell me?" Ashley stared at her father until he looked away.

"What is it, Daddy? Are you going to tell me that Sebastian is a player? That he's been with a lot of women? Is that it? Well, I've got news for you. I am not a virginal schoolgirl. I've had a full life and so has he. Now we want to focus on each other. The past is the past and we are not looking in the rearview mirror. I hope you understand that because I am in love with Sebastian, and I will continue to see him even if you don't like him." She stood and walked around to her father's side. She hugged him tightly and kissed him on the cheek. She did not notice the single tear that escaped his eye.

CHAPTER 15

Sebastian was at the gym when his Apple Watch rang with a familiar number. He had not seen it in nearly two years. The caller ID read MT. He did not answer. He continued lifting weights, honing his already near perfect body. As usual, one or two people who thought they recognized him and two or three people who did indeed recognize him glanced his way. He smiled and nodded to all of them. He showered, changed, headed home and debated whether to call Michael back. He was not ready for the conversation, but he knew it was inevitable.

"We need to talk," Michael said when he answered his phone.

"Okay, I'm listening," Sebastian said.

"No, I don't want to talk about this over the phone. We need to speak in person. This is important."

"I'll text you my address. You can come over now if you want."

Michael arrived in less than an hour. He was wearing a business suit and tie. Sebastian wore a t-shirt and sweatpants.

"You didn't have to dress up for the occasion," he said.

"Fuck you, I had a meeting with some clients."

"Hold up. Relax."

"Relax? You must be joking. You expect me to relax?"

Sebastian opened the door widely and beckoned Michael to sit down on the couch. Sebastian sat in a chair across from him.

"Would you like a drink?"

"No, I do not want a drink. What I want is for you to stay away from my daughter."

"No, Michael. I can't do that. I won't do that. I love Ashley and she loves me."

"Have you gone mad, man? Surely you can see that you have to let her go."

Sebastian leaned forward in his chair. He looked directly into Michael's eyes.

"I don't see that at all. I am a single man, and she is a single woman. We want the same things out of life. We care about each other. We can have a future together."

"How can you even say that? I know your history. I know what you're really like."

"Do you really, Michael? Do you really know me? And if you answer yes, please explain how I am any different from you."

"I do not want my daughter to be with a man who fucks other men. That should be obvious."

"You mean you don't want her to be with a man like her father? Come on, Mike. She will never know unless you tell her. And how will you explain to her just how you know?"

"I can make your life miserable, Sebastian."

"How will you do that, Mike? This is the 21st century, no one really gives a shit about men sleeping with men anymore. If you think exposing me as a bisexual man will ruin my career, think again. There are openly gay men and women on all the major networks now. But if you go there, people will want to know how you know. How will you explain it without exposing yourself? You have way more to lose than I have. I'm a 34-year-old single man living my best life. You on the other hand are a closeted black man in your 50's living in the bible belt. You've been cheating on your wife with men for over 30 years. You will have a lot of explaining to do. Don't push my back against the wall. You will not win. I advise you to do your best imitation of Denzel Washington and act like you like me."

Michael sunk deeper into the couch and covered his face with his hands. His body shuddered. He was wracked with tears. Sebastian moved from his chair and put his arms around him. He held him tightly until the crying ceased.

CHAPTER 16

"I'm so happy," Ashley told her friend, Kirk. "I keep waiting for the other shoe to drop. It always does." They walked arm in arm in a park with Kirk's Cocker Spaniel, Pearl, leading the way on her leash.

"Maybe not this time. You both seem happy together. Maybe this is the one. Even Molly found happiness on Insecure." Ashley squeezed her friend's arm a little tighter as they walked.

"And I'm happy to say Daddy is finally coming around. He's warming up to Sebastian a little."

"I'm not surprised that it took him a while. Sebastian is the first man you've dated that offered Mr. Turner some serious competition. He's handsome, taller than your dad, smart. Nobody will be ever good enough, but it probably makes your dad just a wee bit jealous of him, don't you think?"

"Maybe, but things are looking brighter now."

"Are you and Sebastian talking about a future together?"

"Not in any concrete way but abstractly we have?"

"An abstract future, eh? Sounds interesting?"

Ashley smiled to herself and then brightened.

"Speaking of the future. Work is going great. Have you heard of Abby Oduko?"

"No, who is Abby Oduko?"

"She's a portrait artist. She's Nigerian but born and raised in London. She's based in Chicago now. Her work is all the rage. The portraits sell for megabucks. She even did a commissioned work of Michelle Obama's mother for their house in Cape Cod. Well, guess what? She likes my work. She wants to build a lakefront property in Illinois, and she is considering me to design it."

"That's amazing, Ash. Congratulations."

"Well, I don't have the job yet. She'll look at other architects, of course. But I'm excited about the opportunity. I'm going to Chicago to meet with her next week."

Kirk googled Abby Oduko when he got home. Her website depicted a petite, brown skinned woman with a huge afro and multiple piercings on her nose and lips. She was quite striking. Both arms were sleeved in tattoos. Her artwork was extraordinary. Her portraits featured her subjects surrounded by flowers or vines, their faces rendered in a hyper realistic fashion. The effect was surreal and quite magnificent.

When Ashley shared the news of her meeting with Abby with Sebastian, he said "I know Abby Oduko. She's a tiny woman with a huge personality. You'll like her."

"Did you date her?"

"No, she's just a friend. I prefer a tall drink of water." He kissed Ashley playfully on the cheek.

"Good," Ashley said.

"Would you like me to call Abby for you? I don't know that it would do any good. We weren't that close, but I don't mind doing it."

"No, not now. This is just a first meeting. We'll see how it goes."

CHAPTER 17

Abby Oduko arrived at the Chicago office of MT Architecture in a whirlwind. She was barely 5 feet tall and wore a huge orange faux fur coat that seemed to swallow her whole. Her wild afro had been tamed by a multicolored knit hat and she wore oversized square red eyeglasses. Underneath the flamboyant coat, she was dressed in a sleek black turtleneck sweater, black jeans, and thigh high black suede boots.

She relinquished the standard business handshake when she saw Ashley and pulled her into an enthusiastic bear hug. Ashley took a seat behind her desk and Abby sat in the chair across from her.

"It's a pleasure to meet you, my darling," she said. "Your picture on your website does not do you justice. You are much more beautiful in person."

"As are you," Ashley said.

"I would love to sketch you sometime," Abby said. She rose from her seat abruptly to look closely at Ashley. "You have great cheekbones."

"Thanks, that would be great," Ashley said.

"Well, we can talk about it later. I'm British so we can save the small talk for later. How should we proceed, my dear?"

"Well, I'd like to know about the site where you want to build and what your vision is. Let's go into the conference room where we can spread out and maybe do some sketches."

"Yes, let's," Abby said.

After two hours in the conference room talking about Abby's ideas for her lake house, the women emerged with dinner plans for the next night and a tacit agreement that Ashley would design the house.

Ashley called her father. "We don't have a contract yet, but I feel really good about this. I like Abby and I'm pretty sure she likes me. And she seemed to like my ideas for the house."

"What's not to like, sweetheart? I think you got this. I had a feeling you and Abby would hit it off."

Ashley was so energized; she walked the twelve blocks back to her hotel in the nippy Chicago evening air. She ordered room service, pulled on some comfortable sweats, and opened up her laptop in bed. She went to Abby's website again to compare her photo to the real Abby. She followed her on Twitter and Instagram where she had 450k followers. On her Instagram page, she scrolled down through postings of her artwork, family shoutouts, a photo with Prince Harry and Meghan Markle and another with Oprah. Finally, she focused on a series of photos from a gallery showing three years prior. One picture caught her attention. It was a group shot and Abby was surrounded by several people smiling widely for the camera. Ashley recognized two of the people in the photo. One of them was Sebastian and the other one was her father. Sebastian towered over Abby behind her. It was obvious he was laughing as he lowered his chin into her wild and thick hair. Her father stood next to Sebastian and the camera froze the slight smile on his face and his hand lightly resting on Sebastian's shoulder.

Ashley read the caption underneath the photo. **Good friends sharing my joy at the new Vincent gallery in NYC. Loved it!** The photo was liked by 40,128 people. Ashley went to Sebastian's page on Instagram. He had 8,623 followers and 590 posts. She scrolled through every one of them looking for a picture of her father. She did not find one.

Ashley met Abby at a hip new West African restaurant the next night.

"I really hope you like this place," Abby said. "The food is pretty spicy but the jollof rice is outstanding." She took Ashley's arm as they were led to their table. When they sat down, Abby asked "Is everything okay, love? You seem a little bit distracted." She took Ashley's hand and turned to the waiter when he approached the table.

"Bring us a bottle of that nice Cab I like, please" she said.

"Of course, I'll be right back," the waiter said.

"Okay, spill it, darling. Something is on your mind. What is it?"

"How well do you know Sebastian Campbell?" Ashley asked.

"Pretty well, actually. He was one of the first people I met when I came to Chicago. He's a good friend." Abby looked at Ashley. Her face was placid, drained of the joy and playfulness it exhibited last night.

"Are you shagging him?" Ashley looked down. "Of course, you are." Abby answered her own question. "Why wouldn't you? Sebastian is amazing. Of course, you're fucking him. Why not?" Abby took Ashley's hand in hers. "Ashley dear, if you are worried about me, you can forget it. Sebastian is a lovely, dear man. But he is hardly my type. I prefer my men a little rougher around the edges. Tatted up with a pocket full of edibles. We are just mates. Honestly."

"That is definitely not Sebastian," Ashley said. "He is way too proud of his body to put poisons in it. I just don't know a lot about what his life was like here in Chicago. He doesn't talk about his friends here too much. Look it wouldn't matter if you had dated Sebastian, Abby. I'm not naïve. I know everyone has a past. I'm a grown woman. I get that."

"Of course, you are right to wonder, love. But I wouldn't worry about it too much. Last time I talked to him, he was very happy in Houston. He loves his new job. And now that he's met you, I'm sure he's even more delighted." The waiter arrived with their wine and poured two glasses. "Now let's have a look at this menu," Abby said.

CHAPTER 18

Abby Oduko met Sebastian in much the same way he met Michael Turner. He interviewed her for the CBS affiliate in Chicago. She'd accepted a position to teach art at the School of the Art Institute of Chicago. She was a big "get" for the Institute and the profile Sebastian did of her got picked up by CBS Morning News. They became fast friends and before long they were running in the same circles. And true to her word to Ashley, they were never lovers. Simply friends.

Abby and Sebastian had known each other for about a year, when she called to ask him to be her escort for dinner party at the home of a wealthy art collector.

"I know it will be boring as hell darling, but I bloody well have to go. I need you to come to keep me amused so I don't fall asleep between courses. What do you say?"

"Sure, why not?" he said. "Count me in."

They arrived at the party looking smashing. As luck would have it, they had both chosen gold tones for their evening attire. Abby wore a gold satin mini dress and 6 inch red bottomed heels.

Her hair had golden strands threaded through braids. Sebastian wore a bronze-colored silk jacket with a black shirt and black pants.

When Abby saw him, she said "You look totally fuckable tonight Sebastian. Indeed. Why haven't we done that yet?"

"Because we don't want to ruin this good thing we have."

"I couldn't agree more."

He kissed her on the cheek, and they entered the party arm in arm. The hostess, a tall dark-haired woman with an open, friendly face greeted them gushing, "I'm so happy you're here. Come in and have a cocktail, please." They chatted for a minute before she fluttered away.

"I see the other token over there. We should go and introduce ourselves. I give them credit they found three of us." Abby laughed and took a sip of her cocktail. She nodded her head toward the tall distinguished looking black man in the corner. It was Michael Turner. He was talking animatedly to a slender Asian woman whom Abby recognized.

"Oh, he's talking to Susan Lee. She's a decorator. I know her. She's fun. Let's barge in." They crossed the room. Susan and Abby hugged. The men shook hands.

"This is Michael Turner," Susan said.

"We've met," Sebastian said. "Good to see you again, Michael. I hope things are going well with your business."

"I'm happy. I think Chicago was a good move for us. I'm glad we opened the office."

During dinner, Abby whispered to Sebastian, "Fancy going to that new jazz club on the southside, Pearl's, I think it's called."

"Why not? The night is still young. Let's do it."

"We should invite Brother Michael too. What do you think?"

"Great idea."

An hour later, the three of them were in an Uber headed to Pearl's. They laughed and joked about what a burden it was to be a token. Abby was an accomplished mimic and she had the hostess art patron's Midwestern accent down pat.

"I am so woke. As you can see I have not one but three black friends," she mocked.

"And they are all amazing," Michael chimed in.

The band at the club was very good and the featured singer reminded them all of Jill Scott. They drank and talked about the art world, music, politics and life in America.

"Don't think for a minute that you Yanks have a monopoly on bigots. The British can make it very hard to be West Indian or African or Pakistani in the UK. Racism is a well-seasoned dish served everywhere," Abby said. "And on that depressing note, I should probably be getting home. I have an early morning with a potential client. Someone I met at the party actually. So I take back all the catty things I've said about Jennifer. If not for her party, I might not have a new gig. America is indeed the land of opportunity. And I had a blast with you two. We must do this again soon." The three friends stood and walked out of the club together. The two men each took one of Abby's arms. They stood outside on the empty street.

"How much longer before the car comes?" Abby asked.

"8 minutes," Sebastian said.

"I'm sorry fellows, but I think I need to run back in for a pee."

"No problem, we'll wait for you. Go ahead."

Abby turned and went back into the club. When she got to the ladies' room door, there were two other women waiting ahead of her. She decided she could hold it until she got home after all, and she headed for the door. She walked out but stopped short when she saw Michael and Sebastian. They were facing the street. Their backs were to her. She saw Michael turn slightly to Sebastian touching his face. It was a gesture that was loving and so intimate. Abby stepped back a little into the shadow of the club entrance. They did not see her. Sebastian leaned in and kissed Michael on the lips. He squeezed his hand and then they stepped away from each other creating space as they waited for her to come out of the club.

"I am ready to roll, Gentlemen," Abby called out. And Michael and Sebastian turned to face her, both smiling widely.

CHAPTER 19

Ashley picked over her dinner while Abby ate robustly. "I'll have the apple tart," she told the waiter. "With ice cream of course."

"Abby, I need to ask you about something," Ashley said.

"Ask me anything, darling. What is it?"

"How well did my father know Sebastian before he moved to Houston?" Abby feigned intense interest in her dessert before she spoke. She looked up to see Ashley staring at her intently. She took yet another bite of the tart.

"I saw them in a photo on your Instagram page. You all were at a gallery opening in New York City. It looked like you were having a lot of fun. You referred to them as friends. I got the feeling you had a connection."

"Ashley, darling, I post so many shots on Instagram. I can't remember all of them."

"Would it help if I show you the photo?" She started scrolling on her phone.

Resigned, Abby said, "No, I remember the picture you're talking about. You don't have to show it to me."

"My father and Sebastian claimed they were meeting for the first time when I introduced them in Houston. I know that's a lie, but I don't understand why."

"Ashley, Chicago is a very social town. People don't count casual acquaintances as friends. My God, half the time we don't remember who we meet. People are shallow as fuck. Me especially. I couldn't even tell you the names of all the men I've shagged since I've been here."

"I get the feeling that there's something I'm missing. There's a reason they didn't tell me they knew each other. There's some bad blood there and I want to find out why. My father behaved very badly when he found out I was dating Sebastian. It was just not like him. There is something he is not telling me."

"Ashley, my advice is to let this rest. If your father is okay with things now, why not just let it go? Enjoy your time with Sebastian. People always have in-law issues, and they just adapt and live their lives. Do you love Sebastian?"

"Yes, I do."

"Then please don't go looking for trouble. Just go home and move forward with your man. And stay off social media. It was invented by the devil himself." She smiled at Ashley, but Ashley could not bring herself to smile back.

Later back at her apartment, Abby called Sebastian. He was in a deep sleep and almost did not answer until he realized it was her. He went to bed at 8:00 PM on weeknights.

"I am so sorry to wake you darling, but this could not wait." Sebastian sat up alert now.

"What is it, Abby?"

"I had dinner with Ashley tonight. She knows that you and Michael knew each other in Chicago. She has a lot of questions for you. I tried to blow it off, but I just wanted to prepare you. She is going to ask you about it."

"What did you tell her?"

"I told her people run into people all the time. Chicago is a big city. You can't be bothered to remember everybody you meet. There is truth in that. But remember when we all went to New York for the Vincent opening?"

"Yeah, what does not have to do with anything?"

"There's a picture on my IG page with you, me, Michael and some other people. Well, she found the photo and we all look like fast friends including you and Michael. It puts the lie to the story that you had never met."

"Shit. Thanks for letting me know, Abby. You're a good friend."

"No problem, darling. You know I've always got your back. One question. Do you love her?"

"I do. I love her so much."

"Then why not try the truth?"

"Because the truth will hurt too much," he said.

"Hurt who?"

"Everybody."

CHAPTER 20

Ashley headed straight to Sebastian's house from the airport. She felt like her car was on autopilot. She could not recall a minute of the hour-long drive. Sebastian saw her turn her BMW into the driveway. He raised the garage door so she could park but she didn't seem to notice. She left her phone and her purse on the front passenger seat and walked to the front door. Her mind was racing. She felt detached from her body.

Sebastian opened the door and took her into his arms. He soaked in her scent of coffee and vanilla. He tried to kiss her, but she spoke before his lips could touch hers.

"Why didn't you tell me you knew my father in Chicago? Why did you lie to me?"

"I never lied to you. You never asked me."

"That's bullshit and you know it is. You omitted the facts. That is the same as lying in my book."

"Let's sit down and talk about this, please." He took her arm to lead her to sit on the couch, but she pulled her arm away. She followed into the living room, and they sat down together.

"So, tell me the truth. Did you and Daddy know each other in Chicago?" She looked up at Sebastian. He could see the beginnings of bags under her eyes. She looked unkempt. Her makeup was smudged.

"Yes, we knew each other," Sebastian said. "I wrote a freelance article about him when he first came to Chicago. I saw him from time to time after that. Abby Oduko and I were friends. I ran into him a few times when I was hanging out with her. I just knew him in passing. That's all."

"Then why was he so rude to you when he saw us together? Surely, there's more to the story. I just don't get it."

"You'll have to ask him about that, Ashley. He's just a very protective father. That's all there is to it. I'd be lying if I told you I didn't have a reputation for partying in Chicago. Your dad reacted as any dad would have. He would rather see you with a man with no past. But that man does not exist."

He took Ashley's hand. He could feel her relaxing a bit. He kissed her hand. He kissed her forehead and her cheeks and finally her lips. He sensed the tension being released from her body as he held her in his arms. She kissed him back. She could not help herself.

"I just have one question. Did you come to the Rice Alumnae party specifically to meet me?"

"No. It was just a very lucky break for me. You were there. And you were so beautiful. So amazing. I wanted you from the moment I saw you, but I did not go there looking for you." Ashley sighed with relief. Her face softened. She relaxed.

Sebastian pushed Ashley gently back onto the couch. He unbuttoned her shirt slowly, methodically. He slipped it off her shoulders. He unhooked her bra, freeing her breasts. She pulled his t-shirt over his head. Sebastian took one of Ashley's breasts into his mouth. He sucked and bit bringing her to the threshold of pain. He unzipped her pants and pulled her panties and jeans off, dropping them to the floor. He unzipped his own pants and stripped, leaving his own jeans and underwear in the pile on the floor. His dick was hard and throbbing. He slid one of the decorative couch pillows under her hips and raised her legs over his shoulders before he plunged inside of her wetness.

She threw back her head and screamed "Yes, yes, Oh My God, yes." When she came, she clung to his butt, trying to pull him into an unfathomable depth. He plunged as deeply as he could, holding her hands in his until his juices flowed at first into her and finally onto the space they shared, sweaty, steamy and satiated.

CHAPTER 21

Michael and Rosalinda had been married for fifteen years. By now they were living in the second home they had purchased during their married life. Their children were happy and well adjusted. They were living the American dream. Michael's business was booming. The Chicago office was still a dream, but he was expanding the Houston office. He hired a young architect who was a recent graduate of the University of Texas. His name was Darius Adams. Darius was quite talented and just as charming. He was a good-looking man, very trim, 23 years old.

Like any good businessman's wife, Rosalinda invited Darius over for dinner. He was quite an engaging young man. He raved about the dinner and even interacted well with the children. She liked Darius. It grew late in the evening and Michael said, "I want to show Darius some prints I have in my office, honey. I'll be up in a minute." He kissed his wife.

"Don't keep Darius too long, sweetheart. He came for dinner, not to work. Show him the prints at the office."

"We won't be long. I promise."

"Everything was wonderful, Mrs. Turner. Thank you for dinner," Darius said.

"I'm so glad you enjoyed it. Pleased come again." She kissed her husband and retired for the evening taking the children upstairs with her.

Later she woke up surprised to see that Michael had not joined her in bed. She sat straight up at looked at the clock on the bedside table. It was 12:45 AM. She pulled on her robe and walked to the top of the stairs. She did not hear voices or movement. She grew concerned and walked into the living room and kitchen. It was then that she heard laughter coming from Michael's office. She approached the office door. She did not knock, and the door was unlocked. She opened the door to see Michael sitting in his office chair. He was wearing just his shirt. He was nude from the waist down and young Darius Adams was completely nude and sucking Michael's dick with gusto.

"Michael, Michael. Oh my God," she screamed. She ran out of the room and up to her bedroom and locked the door. Michael followed her upstairs. She heard Darius' car engine start and he drove away.

"Rosie, open the door, please. Please, Rosie." Michael pulled on the doorknob. Rosie would not open the door until she heard the children's voices.

"Mommy, what's going on? Daddy, did something happen?"

Rosalinda opened the door. "Everything is okay, go back to bed," she told the children.

"What happened, Mom? What is it?"

"We'll talk about it in the morning. Please go back to bed."

"But Mom…" Brian said.

"Go to bed now," Michael said. The children went back to their rooms, skeptical. Michael followed Rosie into their bedroom. She stood in the middle of the room with her hands covering her face as she cried.

"At least now I know why you don't want to fuck me," she said. "It all makes sense now." Michael took her into his arms.

"I love you so much, Rosie. Please forgive me. I can't explain it … it's sometimes I like …"

He was crying now. His body shook. They held each other tightly.

"Please don't leave me, Rosie. You are my life. You and the kids are the reason I live."

Rosie stiffened and stepped back and looked at him.

"I am not going anywhere," she said. "I like my life. But you listen to me. You have to get rid of that boy. I don't care how you do it. Pay him some money. Do whatever you need to do." She was crying again but trying to keep her voice low. "I don't ever want to see him again."

"Alright, baby. Whatever you say. I'll take care of it tomorrow."

Michael fired Darius Adams and paid him a severance of $15,000 which was quite a sum for a 23-year-old. Darius did not have the sophistication to sue his boss for sexual harassment. He had only worked for one month at MT Architects, so he did not feel compelled to include it on his resume.

The next morning, Ashley asked her mother, "What was happening last night, Mom? Why were you and Daddy fighting?"

"It wasn't a fight, honey. I just wish your dad didn't work so hard. Poor Darius needed to catch a break. I told Daddy to let the poor man have some off time. We shouldn't invite him over for supper and then expect him to work all night. That's all."

Two days after Darius left, Michael closed the clasp of a 7-carat total weight diamond tennis bracelet set in platinum onto Rosalinda's elegant wrist.

"It's beautiful, Michael. Thank you."

CHAPTER 22

"Hello sweetheart, I wasn't expecting you," Rosalinda said. "Why didn't you call me? I would have cooked something." Ashley hugged her mother.

"Don't worry about it, Mom. I just need to talk to Dad about something. I'm not hungry."

"He's in the den. Is everything okay? What's going on?"

"It's nothing, Mom. We can talk later." She headed back to the den.

"How's Sebastian? Are you two still going strong? I think you know how much I like him."

"We're fine, Mom. We're still together?" Ashley looked away from her mother.

"Why am I getting a weird feeling? Did something happen with you two?" Rosalinda took her daughter's hand. "Sit down for a minute," she said. "What?" They sat down at the kitchen island.

"I found out Dad and Sebastian knew each other in Chicago. They both acted like they were meeting for the first time when

Sebastian came over here for dinner. It kind of bothers me that Dad never said anything about it. I think it's strange, don't you?"

"A little. What did Sebastian say about it?"

"He said he and Dad met a couple of times but they weren't really friends. He just assumed Daddy didn't remember him. They were just acquaintances. I just want to hear what Daddy says about it. I'm going to talk to him about it." She stood up and Rosalinda touched her hand.

"Let me know what he says."

Ashley found her father sitting in his favorite chair reading a book. His face brightened when he saw his daughter. He removed his reading glasses and put the book and the glasses down on the ottoman in front of the chair. He stood to embrace his daughter.

"Well, look who's here. It's my baby girl. I thought I heard voices. Sit down, tell me about your Chicago trip. What did you think of Abby?"

"It was a great trip. I liked Abby a lot. She is quite the character."

"She is indeed. Sit down, baby." Michael sat back down in his chair. Ashley removed the book and glasses from the ottoman and sat down across from him. The door to the den was still open. Rosalinda stood just outside the door listening.

"Daddy, why didn't you tell me you and Sebastian knew each other in Chicago?"

Michael leaned back in his chair and looked away from Ashley for a moment before returning her gaze.

"We only met officially once. He wrote a freelance article about me for an architectural magazine. It was no big deal. The Chicago office had just opened, and we were getting a lot of press. After that, I would run into him occasionally. We both knew Abby Oduko so there was that connection. When he came here for dinner, he acted like he didn't remember me, so I played along. It kind of pissed me off actually. I felt disrespected. I think you can recall I did not behave like a gentleman that night."

"I do remember that. I was really disappointed in you. It was so unlike you."

Michael leaned forward and took his daughter's hands in his.

"I know, baby. And I'm sorry. Now, can't we get past this? I just want you to be happy and if Sebastian makes you happy, I support you 100%." He took Ashley into his arms and kissed her cheek.

"Thank you, Daddy. I'm tired. I think I am going to go home and sleep the rest of the weekend away. I'll see you in the office on Monday."

"Okay, Sweetheart." Michael stood and took his daughter's arm. Rosalinda retreated to the kitchen where she poured herself a glass of wine.

"I'm leaving, Mom. I'm tired. I'll call you tomorrow." Ashley kissed her parents goodbye and left the kitchen, letting herself out of the front door.

When Ashley was gone, Rosalinda and Michael sat at the kitchen island in silence for a few minutes. Finally, Rosalinda spoke "So am I right to assume that Sebastian was one of your fuck boys in Chicago?" She looked at Michael, but his eyes were closed. His hands were steepled in front of his face as if in prayer.

"No, Rosie. It wasn't like that."

"Then what was it like?"

"He was a friend. He wasn't a fuck boy." Michael could not bring himself to look directly at this wife.

"Oh, my God. You loved him. Didn't you?" Rosalind pulled Michael's hands away from his face. "Look at me," she demanded. "You still love him, don't you? Answer me. You're in love with him. Aren't you?" Michael bowed his head and the tears flowed. His and Rosalinda's.

"Stop crying, Michael. You're a sorry excuse for a man and an even sorrier father. It's a new day. Gay marriage is legal now. You can divorce me and marry Sebastian if you want to. I really don't give a shit what you do. But listen to me and listen carefully. You are going to make sure that Ashley and Sebastian end their relationship. I don't care how you do it. It's no skin off my back if you tell Ashley about you and Sebastian. It will break her heart, but I will be there to comfort her. I just know I want better for her than what I have. I don't want her to spend her life wondering who her husband is fucking and what kind of STDs he is bringing into her house. She will not be bought off by the occasional diamond bracelet or a trip to Bali. She is better than I am. She is an educated accomplished woman. I had no education, no career and no money of my own. My daughter deserves better. Do you hear me, Michael? Do you hear me?" She stood and took Michael by the shoulders and shook him harshly. He nodded.

"I hear you," he said.

Chapter 23

Michael Turner appeared to be a 54-year-old man in the picture of health. He was tall and lean, well within the healthy weight range for his height and age. His blood pressure and cholesterol were all within acceptable targets. He ate healthy foods and drank in moderation. He played golf and worked out at the gym 3 times a week. He did not smoke except for the occasional cigar. He was wealthy so he did not worry about money or the legacy he would leave for his family. But he was a closeted gay man who had been in therapy for years. His mental health was not good. He had never been able to be his true self and it had taken a toll on him. He was mentally exhausted from playing a role which society had forced him to play. He had lived a life of fear and self-loathing. Now he would finally come out. And he would do it with his daughter, Ashley. He would do it to save her.

Ashley rang the buzzer to enter her parents' gated community. Her father buzzed her into the subdivision of sprawling brick homes that backed up to either a manmade lake or the golf course. The houses all had either 3 or 4 car detached garages. The Turner house was one of the lakefront properties. It had been designed by Michael Turner and the interior was carefully curated by Rosalinda Olivares Turner. When Ashley turned into the driveway, she saw her father sitting outside on the patio with a drink in his hand. He did not immediately look at her when she approached him.

"Hey, Daddy. What's going on? How are you doing?"

"I'm alright, baby. Come sit down." He patted the chair next to his.

"You're making me nervous. Tell me what's going on with you. Where is Mom?"

"Your mother is in the house. I wanted to talk to you about something before you speak with your mother."

"What is it? Are you ill? Is there something the matter with Mom?" Ashley sat on the edge of the orange cushioned seat. Michael leaned forward with his elbows on his knees.

"I probably should have had Brian here too." He looked Ashley squarely in the face and said, "I'm gay. I am a gay man. I have loved your mother for over 30 years but physically I prefer men. I was born this way, Ashley. It's taken a lot of therapy for me to get to the point that I could say this out loud, but I am finally here, and I am praying that you can accept me. I am still your father and I love you more than life." He reached for her hands. She looked at his hands as though they were foreign objects. Her throat was dry. She could not speak. She thought for a minute that she had not heard the words. She began to gasp for breath. Michael pulled her into his arms. He squeezed her and patted her the back.

"I'll get you some water." He ran into the house and returned with the bottle of water. Ashley was bent over with her head between her legs, still hyperventilating. He handed her the water, and she drank it thirstily.

"Does Mom know?" she asked hoarsely.

"She does now. She's always suspected it. But you have to understand, it took me years to even admit it to myself. I didn't choose this. I tried so hard not to be this. Young people today can be more open. I couldn't do it. I thought if I didn't claim them, the feelings would go away. But they didn't. They never did." He sat back down in the chair and Ashley stood up and put her arms around him. He cried until his body was wracked with tears and Ashley cried with him.

"Are you and Mom staying together? What will happen to our family?"

"We will stay together. I still love your mother and she loves me. We are still your family, Ashley. That will never change."

Ashley wiped her tears and said, "Then I guess I will have to learn to live with your truth. You're still my father. I still love you with all of my heart."

"Then let's go inside. There is something else we need to talk about."

They walked arm in arm into the house and into the kitchen where Rosalinda was sitting at the kitchen table. Ashley embraced her mother and held her tightly without speaking. Michael sat down next to her, and Ashley sat across from them. A look passed between Rosalinda and Michael that Ashley noticed but could not decipher. Rosalinda squeezed Michael's hand.

"Mom, are you alright?" Ashley asked.

"Yes, I'm fine but there is something else we all need to talk about." She nodded at Michael, and he looked away unable to make eye contact with either of them.

Finally, he spoke. "You asked me how well I knew Sebastian in Chicago. I wasn't honest with you, Ashley and neither was he." Ashley's eyes widened. She felt the warmth evaporate from her body.

"What are you saying? Tell me, please."

"Sebastian and I were lovers. We were together for almost four years." Rosalinda flinched. Michael reached for Ashley's hand, but she snatched it away. Rosalinda rose from her chair to support her daughter, thinking she looked faint. The color drained from her face. Her spine felt like jelly and Michael too rose to support her. She was slipping to the floor, so Michael picked her up carried her and lay her down on the living room couch. Rosalinda ran cool water on a dish towel and used it to wipe her face. Michael and Rosalinda both kneeled on the floor next to their daughter.

"I had not seen Sebastian in over a year when he came to Houston. I thought we had cut the ties forever. So, when I saw him with you, I lost it. I couldn't believe it. I didn't want him to hurt you, but I felt exposed too. And I've been running away from that feeling for 30 years."

Ashley looked at her parents. Her father looked diminished, smaller, older. Rosalinda looked away; her face pained but determined. Her expression was steely. The pleasant friendly countenance had disappeared. She spoke directly to Ashley as if Michael was not even in the room.

"Your father will contact Sebastian and tell him. You can't continue to see him. He can't be trusted. You do understand, don't you?"

Ashley closed her eyes tightly forcing more tears to fall. She turned her face away from her parents and said "I understand. But you shouldn't be the one to tell him. I have to do it myself."

CHAPTER 24

Ashley watched from her window as Sebastian approached her house for what would be the last time. The sight of him made her breathless as it had ever since she met him. She opened the door before he had a chance to ring the bell. He pulled her into an embrace and kissed her as he always did but he could feel the tension that was pervasive in her body.

"Hey, babe. What's up? You sounded strange when you called."

"Come in. Let's sit down." He followed her to the couch where she waited for him to sit. She sat down leaving space between them. He moved closer to her, but she held up her hands to stop him.

"What's going on, Ash?"

"I know about you and Daddy. He told me you were lovers in Chicago." Ashley looked directly at Sebastian. He did not look away. He did not recoil.

He faced her straightaway and said, "I won't lie to you. We did have a relationship. Your father is an amazing man. He is kind and funny. I don't have to tell you. He is brilliant and generous. We had a good time but there was no way we could have a future together. Your father is of the generation that is more comfortable on the down low. That is not me. I am who I am."

"What do you mean 'that is not you'? That's exactly you. Isn't that what you're doing?" Ashley's face grew hot with anger. She stared Sebastian down. He still did not flinch.

"No, it isn't. I have slept with men and women. I won't lie to you about that. I love the person, not the body they inhabit. That doesn't matter to me. I once loved your father and now I love you with all my heart." He reached for her hand. She did not pull away.

"I could never trust you. I would always suspect you would leave me for a man," Ashley said.

"How is that any different from any other committed relationship? If one person wants out, what does it matter if they leave for another man or another woman? They just want to leave. Well, I don't want out. I want to stay. I love you Ashley and I think you love me too. We could make this work. I know we could." He pulled her into his arms and kissed her deeply. She was crying now.

"I can't do this," she said. "It's too much. My parents are at a crossroads. My brother isn't taking any of this well. He is heartbroken. I have to help my family get through this. You need to go." She sat up abruptly, pulling herself out of his embrace.

"Look at me and tell me you don't love me," Sebastian demanded.

Ashley looked away and stood up.

"Please go," she said.

Sebastian stood and said, "You can't do it, can you? You know you love me. You can't tell me you don't." He touched her face and kissed her forehead. "I'll leave, but not without telling you how much I adore you. I love you more than I have ever loved anyone. I can't imagine my life without you. If you change your mind, I will come back to you in a heartbeat." He hugged her again feeling the familiarity of her body against his. She did not pull away from him. He wanted to kiss her, but she could not offer her lips. He kissed her on her cheek one last time and then left. He did not look back. Ashley watched him from her window as he climbed into his car and drove away.

EPILOGUE

ichael and Rosalinda Turner rented a luxury villa in Ibiza to celebrate their 32nd wedding anniversary. They were surrounded by family and friends. Their daughter Ashley and son Brian were there. Brian came with his new fiancé Chelsea and Ashley's best friend Kirk and her girlfriend Makayla were also there. Michael paid for his staff from the Houston and Chicago offices to join them as well. The week was a beautiful celebration for a loving couple. The guests who had lovers clung to them closely while the others dreamed of such a perfect union.

Brian offered a toast raising his champagne glass, "Wishing at least 32 more years of joy and happiness to my amazing parents who met on the subway in New York City. May your love continue to grow and may you always lead us all by your example of kindness and grace. Happy Anniversary, Mom and Dad!"

"Happy Anniversary," everyone chimed in. As Michael and Rosalinda leaned in to kiss each other, Ashley made her own silent toast.

"May you each find your inner peace and acceptance. Live truthfully and out loud. Only then will you really be happy."

While the Turners and friends celebrated on an island in the Mediterranean, Sebastian Campbell focused on his career. He had been promoted to an evening news anchor and nominated for a daytime Emmy Award. He worked out regularly at the gym and started meditating. He did volunteer work with a suicide prevention group. He felt he was becoming a better person. And he dreamed of winning Ashley back. He truly believed it would happen. In his heart, he had faith in the power of their mutual attraction. He loved her and she loved him. And he would wait as long as he needed to because he was nothing if not a patient man.

ABOUT THE AUTHOR

Azalyn St. Francis is a world traveler, poet, wine lover, foodie and community activist. She has published two books of poetry. This is her fourth novella.

Also by Azalyn St. Francis

Best Laid Plans: The Weekend (Book 1 of a Series)
Best Laid Plans: The Aftermath (Book 2 of a Series)
The Madison – Cameron Wedding

www.ingramcontent.com/pod-product-compliance
Lightning Source LLC
Chambersburg PA
CBHW051438150726
48000CB00005B/2150